Abby's Wish

Story by Liza St. John
Illustrations by Michael Krone

RSVP

**RAINTREE
STECK-VAUGHN**
P U B L I S H E R S
The Steck-Vaughn Company

Austin, Texas

The time for dedication is here:
For all who've made wishes far and near.
And if for a friend you've wished on a star,
Just be a friend to learn who your true
    friends are.

Thanks to my teachers, Mr. St. John and
    Ms. Crick,
They've stood beside me through the thin and
    the thick;
My family and friends, whose personalities and
    features,
Helped bring to life these small, little creatures;
And Raintree/Steck-Vaughn,
For all the work that they have done. — L.S.J.

To my parents, Betty and Herman. — M.K.

Printed in Mexico.

1 2 3 4 5 6 7 8 9 0 RRD 99 98 97 96 95 94

Library of Congress Cataloging-in-Publication Data

St. John, Liza, 1981-
    Abby's wish / story by Liza St. John; illustrations by Michael Krone.
        p.   cm. — (Publish-a-book)
    Summary: Abby the rabbit wishes she had a friend, as long as it's not funny-looking Horrible Hare.
    ISBN 0–8114–7272–8
    1. Children's writings.   [1. Rabbits — Fiction.
2. Friendship — Fiction.   3. Conduct of life — Fiction.
4. Stories in rhyme.   5. Children's writings.]   I. Krone, Michael, ill.   II. Title.   III. Series.
PZ8.3.S774Ab   1995
[Fic] — dc20   94-40436
                                                      CIP   AC

Down Liza Lane, a winding driveway,
There's a little spot called the Golden Greenway.
Here you would find forest animals all
Playing games with each other from spring until fall.

4

One of these youngsters, a wee little bunny,
Was Abby the rabbit, who liked to be funny.
Abby loved to play at this grassy green knoll;
And here starts the story you're about to be told.

Wishes and dreams filled this small rabbit's head
From stories she read before going to bed.
The stories would tell her how genies would say,
"I'll grant you three wishes; wish what you may."

She read books about magic, wishes, and such;
Stories of happiness, superstitions, and luck.
So Abby would spend day after day
Wishing for a friend with whom she could play.

At night she would look and wish on a star,
Hoping a friend would come from afar.
But a friend for poor Abby never did come her way,
Even though she wished for one, day after day.

There were other animals she could play with, of course,
Like Sneaky Snake and Hateful Horse,
Cantankerous Cat and Boastful Bat,
Horrible Hare and Backstabbing Rat.

13

Now Horrible Hare was a sight to behold,
If there was ever a joke, on him it was told.
Adolescence was the culprit, the rascal, you see.
(Someday this guy will get you and me!)

Fuzzy and frizzy, unruly, his hair
Made Horrible look a lot like a bear.
He had two new front teeth with which he could eat;
It seemed they were almost as large as his feet.

When the forest animals were all in a crowd,
Abby made fun of Horrible out loud.
Poor Horrible was really quite kind;
All his bad traits were in Abby's mind.

Abby wanted to be the center of attention,
So she made Horrible suffer great affliction.
She strapped on her feet two small canoes,
And into her mouth went two large kazoos.

She said, "Guess who I am! Hey, look at me!"
Everyone looked and laughed, "Ha ha! Hee hee!"
Everyone except poor Horrible Hare,
Who hung his head low and sobbed with despair.

Off Abby went — hippity hop —
Up the side of the knoll, straight to the top,
Making fun of poor Horrible in every way,
Poking fun at him nearly all day.

20

Abby jumped over a log and slipped on a rock,
Rolled down the hill, hit her head with a knock.
She was so embarrassed she thought she would die.
She opened her mouth and let out a sigh.

At the top of the knoll, next to a tree,
Horrible moved to the edge so he could see.
Before this, for Abby, Horrible had no respect,
But seeing her hurt had a tremendous effect.

Horrible stood up with a new sense of pride
And put all his bad feelings for Abby aside.
He decided right then Abby would be his best friend.
A friendship like this one never would end.

Afraid of what all the animals would say,
Abby tried to hide from them the next day.
But early that morning, it must have been eight,
Abby heard someone come through the gate.

Then her mom said, "Oh, please do come in."
Abby didn't know it, but she had made her first friend.
There stood Horrible Hare at her bedroom door,
With an armload of books and games galore.

Day after day Horrible took care of Abby;
She had no reason to be the least bit crabby.
Abby had thought that Horrible was unbearable,
But now she realized it was she who had been terrible.

Abby saw Horrible in a different light now;
His teeth and his feet weren't as big somehow.
She picked up her hairbrush and told Horrible, "Sit";
His fur was much longer, not nearly as thick.

Abby learned a great lesson, one not in her books.
A friend is a friend not judged by their looks.
Wishes are fine, and dreams might come true,
But to make a friend, be a friend — that's all you have to do.

Just look how Abby and Horrible got through.
If you want, let it be an example for you.
It's good to have dreams and make wishes on stars,
But you should realize that we make the people we are.

Liza St. John, author of **Abby's Wish**, actually lives on Liza Lane, in Morrison, Tennessee. She plays down Liza Lane and the Golden Greenway with her cousins and friends. Being an only child, Liza has a special love for her pets, which have included rabbits, fish, parakeets, hermit crabs, frogs, newts, cats, dogs, and chinchillas.

Liza began her writing career at the age of two when she would dictate stories to her grandmother. Liza's winning story was written as a class assignment when she was in the sixth grade at East Coffee Elementary School in Manchester, Tennessee. She was sponsored in the 1994 Publish-a-Book Contest by her enrichment teacher, Ms. Sherry Crick.

Liza's father, Glen, is a computer technician, and her mother, Debbie, an art teacher. Liza is active in cheerleading, dance, gymnastics, and chorus. She is also an accomplished artist and has won several art contests and local shows. Her newest love is drama, and her goal is to become an actress while maintaining her hobbies in art and writing.

The twenty honorable-mention winners in the **1994 Raintree/Steck-Vaughn Publish-a-Book Contest** were Dennis J. Lee, Bowen School, Newton, Massachusetts; Jessica Stephen, Harborside School, Milford, Connecticut; Cassandra Gaddo, Southview Elementary School, Waconia, Minnesota; Emily Hinson, Robert E. Lee Elementary School, East Wenatchee, Washington; Jessie Manning, Rice Lake Elementary School, Maple Grove, Minnesota; Neil Finfrock, Brimfield Elementary, Kent, Ohio; Andrew Campbell, St. Eugene's School, Santa Rosa, California; Tiffany McDermott, St. Rose of Lima School, Freehold, New Jersey; Laura Dorval, Riverside Middle School, Chattaroy, Washington; Alison Taylor, Fisher Elementary School, Oklahoma City, Oklahoma; Kendra Hennig, East Farms School, Farmington, Connecticut; Lisa Walters, Northeast Elementary School, Kearney, Nebraska; Hunter Stitik, Forest Oak Elementary School, Newark, Delaware; Jamie Pucka, Rensselaer Central Middle School, Rensselaer, Indiana; April Wagner, Monte Vista Middle School, San Jacinto, California; Elizabeth Neale, Clifton Springs Elementary School, Clifton Springs, New York; Rachel Kuehn, Roseville Public Library, Roseville, California; Carolyn Blessing, John Diemer School, Overland Park, Kansas; Kelsey Condra, Grace Academy of Dallas, Dallas, Texas; Michael Gildener-Leapman, Charles E. Smith Jewish Day School, Rockville, Maryland.

Michael Krone was born in DuQuoin, Illinois, and grew up on a farm amidst all kinds of animals. Instilled with a passion for drawing at an early age, he went on to obtain fine arts degrees from the University of Illinois and the University of Florida. He has worked as an illustrator in Miami and Tallahassee, and since 1977 has been a freelance illustrator in advertising and publishing in Austin, Texas.

Liza St. John